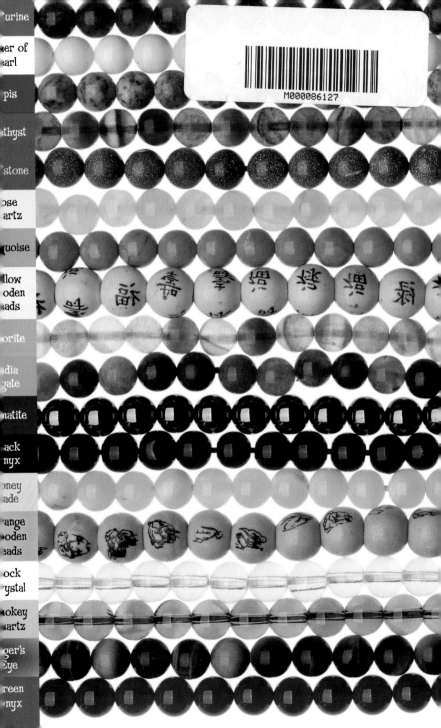

Bead Power!

A Guidebook to Bead Bracelets

By Nancy Krulik

GROSSET & DUNLAP
New York

For Jeffrey and Amy, strong powers in my life —N.K.

Cover and insert photos by Keith Rizza.
Special thanks to Jennifer Frantz and Carl Ferrero.

ISBN 0-448-42291-3   A B C D E F G H I J

Table of Contents

A Bead Bonanza!

What do you wish you had more of: Brains? True love? Money? Serenity? Wouldn't it be awesome if you could find the answers to all of your problems in a beaded bracelet?

The belief that wearing certain gemstones around your wrist can change things in your life is the theory behind power bead bracelets—the wristlets made of round, multi-colored gemstones that everybody is wearing these days.

Okay, so we're not really saying that your dreams will come true the minute you put on a power bead bracelet. But it's fun to think that way, isn't it? And some people really do believe that wearing bracelets and necklaces made with semi-precious stones or carved wooden beads can change their lives in some small way. That's why literally millions of people are donning Buddhist *mala* beads, better known as power beads. (Some people also call them karma beads.)

While we may never know for sure whether or not these beads will bring fame, fortune, wealth, and health to the folks who wear them, one thing is certain: Power beads are having a huge influence on American culture—especially when it comes to fashion.

According to several teen fashion magazines, power bead bracelets are the top accessory on everyone's list. And no one can wear just one. Once you get hooked on wearing power bead bracelets, you have to have more and more of them. Power bead bracelets look and work best when they are worn in pairs or groups of several bracelets.

Where can you find power bead bracelets? Everywhere. You'll see them in the windows at sophisticated department stores like Saks Fifth Avenue, and strewn across card tables at local flea markets. As one buyer for Saks told CNN, "Everyone is buying power beads: all sexes, all ages, across the country. Rarely do you get a trend that appeals to so many people."

Although it may seem like everyone you know has been wearing power beads almost forever, the beaded bangles are a fairly new phenomenon on the American trend-setting scene. It all started with a jewelry designer named Zoe Metro, who began selling her bracelets for twenty to forty dollars in fancy department stores. Zoe got her idea for the bracelets after she saw the Dalai Lama, the spiritual leader of Tibetan Buddhists, wearing his *mala* beads.

At first, people were skeptical. Some even laughed at Zoe's designs. But Zoe has had the last laugh. She's sold thousands of her bracelets. And copies of them are being hawked everywhere—some for as little as one dollar. It seems that everyone wants to wear a power bracelet (or two, or three, or four!).

If you are a power bracelet fan—and these days, who isn't?—then you'll want to get the full scoop on how these little beads work their spiritual magic, and which types of beads will fit your needs. Lucky for you, we've got the info.

This book will increase your knowledge about Buddhist *mala* beads. And that's a good thing. After all, knowledge is power. And power is what these beads are all about!

Where Does the Power Come From?

Power bead bracelets are unique in the jewelry world because they are said to have healing forces that can help you overcome many of life's problems. Each color bead has its own type of healing power. Need an extra boost of brains on test day? Wear an intelligence-building amethyst power bead bracelet. In a hurry to get things done? Place some pale yellow honey jade around your wrist and find patience you never knew you had.

Just how do power beads create such major changes in your life? Well, according to people who study New Age philosophies, it's not actually the beads that do it. Rather, it's the semi-precious stones that the beads are made of that cause the change. According to believers, rocks and stones, because they come from the earth, are filled with life force energy, just like animals and plants are. When you place certain stones near your body, the stone's natural energy affects what's going on in your own chakra, or personal energy center. According to believers, that can alter your emotional, physical, and spiritual well being.

You may be surprised to learn that not all power beads are made of stone. Some are made of wood and can be decorated with carvings of Asian figures, all of which have their own distinct meanings. The wooden beads are also considered to having healing properties. (At one time some *mala* beads were actually carved from human bone. But that practice has long since disappeared, although some people do wear *mala* beads made from animal bones.)

But even if the wooden or gemstone beads you wear around your neck and wrist don't radically alter your life, they do look great. And that's a good enough reason as any to wear them.

The Dalai Lama himself has suggested another purpose you might have for wearing the beads: "There are so many things I don't know. I don't know computers or how to calculate. Sometimes I use my (*mala*) beads for calculations," he recently joked to a group of reporters.

Power beads as math tools? Now there's an idea!

Beads
Through Time

Look around you. Power beads are everywhere. Everyone who is anyone has hitched onto their spiritual wagon. Just check out the members of Hollywood's A-list who are true believers:

Ricky Martin lives his *vida loca* while wearing power beads, onstage and off. Madonna rarely leaves the house without her *mala* bracelets and necklaces. Jennifer Aniston and Brad Pitt have been seen in matching bracelets. Even wild child grunge singer Courtney Love hangs power beads from her microphone when she performs with her band, Hole.

That settles it. Power beads are totally now.

Or are they? It might surprise you to know that beads like this have been around for thousands of years.

Throughout time people have been using beads as part of their religious rituals. In fact, the root for the word bead, *bede*, actually means to pray.

People of many religions have used strands of beads to help them pray and meditate. Tibetan monks have used *mala* beads for centuries as counting tools to keep track of how many prayers they have said.

But beads have been used for more than prayer.

Ever since medieval times, people have looked to stones for their healing powers. In the 1200s, kids didn't go to the pediatrician when flu season hit. Instead, their parents made them wear coral beads to ward off illnesses.

Now here we are, in the beginning of a new millennium. We've got medicines to cure diseases. We travel through space at almost the speed of light. We're part of a computerized world, where everything can be altered with the push of a button. And yet, people are once again turnng to stones in the hopes of changing their lives. Why?

"Americans today are taking a mental account of what is important. They are more mystical and inspirational," Irma Zandl, owner of the Zandl Research group, recently told CNN. "Power beads fit right into that. They are about … feeling good."

Feeling good. Sounds like the perfect reason to pile on the beads and let those positive vibes sink in.

Take a Closer Look

It's not only the stones on power bead bracelets and necklaces that give off positive energy. Some people think that the way the necklaces and bracelets are put together also affects their ability to inspire change. So before you race out and buy yourself just any strand of *mala* beads or a brand-new power bead bracelet, take the time to make sure it's got all the right stuff.

The real *mala* strands—the kinds Tibetan Buddhist monks use—have 108 beads. Each bead on the strand represents one of the earthly desires that humans have. Take a close look at a strand of traditional *mala* beads and you will see that one bead is larger than the rest. That bead, which is called the guru bead, represents Buddha. The guru bead is usually found near the tassel that is formed where both ends of the strand join together to form a circle.

Of course, not everyone wants to walk around with a 108-bead *mala* strand all day. And that's where power bead bracelets come in. But how do you know if you are buying the genuine article? For starters, make sure the stones are genuine, and not plastic copies of actual semi-precious gemstones. The actual gemstones get their power from the earth. Plastic is man-made, and lacks the same energy. Then look to see that there is a guru bead and a tassel where the ends of the strand meet.

However, if you find a bracelet you love but discover that it's missing the guru bead or you're not quite sure if the purple beads are truly amethyst, don't walk away empty-handed. Go ahead and buy the bracelet. Part of the power behind power bracelets comes from your belief that they can work. And remember, if a bracelet, a necklace, or a charm has been lucky for you in the past, keep wearing it. After all, anything that brings you luck or success is powerful to you.

Cracking the Color Code

Okay, so now you know that every stone in a wrist *mala* has its own power. But which stone should you wear on a day when you need a positive attitude? Which of your bracelets should you put on during a day when you feel like you're getting a touch of the flu? And just which semi-precious gemstone beads will give you the self-control you need to keep from screaming at your little brother after you've found him snooping in your room again?

If these are the questions you've been asking yourself, then you've come to the right place. We've got all the answers right here, on the following pages. We've cracked the power bead color code!

Amethyst

Purple

light to dark; transluscent to opaque

Intelligence/Mental Focus

What a night! You were up really late studying for that big history test. But it was worth it. You've finally got all the dates straight in your head, and the spelling of every name is ingrained in your memory forever. Now there's just one more thing you should do to ensure that you'll ace that exam—put on your amethyst power bead bracelet.

Amethyst stones give off an energy that helps your mental focus while boosting your intelligence at the same time. It's a one-two combo that will help you beat the big-test-blues. Think of it as purple power!

Cool Combo

Wear amethyst and rose quartz bracelets together to enhance your newfound intelligence with self-love.

Aventurine

Green
light to dark; mostly opaque
Success / Decision-Making

Okay, you've got a big decision to make today—which of your many power bracelets should you wear? Well, before you make your choice, put on your aventurine bracelet. Aventurine stones have a unique power to help you delve into your natural intuition and become more decisive.

Aventurine's ability to help you make choices has an extra added bonus. Because people respect folks who can make a decision with ease, aventurine wearers often find themselves placed in leadership positions. If you wear aventurine, people will look to you for help and guidance, because you will be able to see things clearly and make choices that can benefit yourself and others.

Cool Combo
Wear aventurine with any other stone, and it will bring you added confidence.

Black Onyx

Jet Black
dark and shiny; opaque

Self-Control / Willpower

Are you the kind of person who makes important resolutions every New Year's Eve—only to break them all by January 3rd? Then here's a resolution you really should keep: wear a black onyx power bead bracelet.

Black onyx *mala* beads will give you the self-control you need to make the changes you want, and to stick with them. These beads can help you keep stay with your new exercise regime, or from forgetting about your vow to study harder in math this year. And when it comes to bettering yourself, there's no greater power than willpower!

Cool Combo

Mix black onyx and fluorite bracelets to rid yourself of negative thoughts while you try to stick to your resolutions.

18

Fluorite

Purple/Grey/Clear/Blue/Green
multi-colored; translucent

Peace / Meditation / Stress Relief

Let's face it. The world can be pretty stressful. Between school, homework, your daily chores, and baby-sitting and your newspaper delivery route, there never seems to be enough hours in a day to do the things you need to do. And forget about doing the things you want to do!

Being stressed all the time isn't healthy for your mind or your body. That's why you need to take some time each day to sit quietly and think peaceful thoughts. But with your busy schedule, just when and how are you supposed to find the time to do that?

Here's your answer: Put on some fluorite beads. Then take a deep breath, and imagine yourself at peace. Fluorite beads improve your ability to meditate on peaceful thoughts. And isn't that just what you could use right about now?

Cool Combo

To increase your feelings of peace and serenity, wear both fluorite and hematite power beads.

Goldstone

Brown/Red/Gold
golden speckles/sparkly; opaque
Self-Confidence/Positive Attitude

Here's the secret to success: You have to believe in yourself. The biggest difference between winners and losers is that winners really believe that they belong in the winner's circle.

But positive self-esteem isn't always easy to come by. So, on those days when you're feeling less than confident, put on a goldstone power bracelet and face the world. Goldstone infuses your energy center with a totally positive attitude. And sometimes that's all you need to help you grab that brass ring.

Cool Combo

Wear mother of pearl and goldstone bracelets together to direct that positive energy to financial gains.

Green Onyx

Green
deep and shiny; opaque

Positive Self-Esteem Energy

If green goes better with your outfit than golden brown, trade in your goldstone for green onyx power beads. Like goldstone, green onyx beads boost your self-esteem and foster self-love. And just imagine what you can achieve if you wear green onyx and goldstone together— you'll be unstoppable!

Cool Combo

Mix and match your green onyx and smokey quartz power bead bracelets to rid yourself of any negativity, allowing the positive self-image to totally take over.

Hematite

Silver/Black

dark and shiny, metallic-looking; opaque

Healing/Balance

To rid yourself of depression, put on a set of hematite power beads. Not only will they help heal your broken spirit, but some people believe that they can heal your body as well. Certain hematite stones have a unique magnetic property that may rid your body of aches and pains. This dual power helps you achieve a positive balance between your body and your mind.

Cool Combo

Wear hematite bracelets with honey jade to give you the patience you need to deal with the trials of your day.

If you have a friend who's all achy with a cold or the flu, think about sending over a hematite bracelet with the chicken soup. It will give "get well soon" a whole new meaning!

Honey Jade

Yellow

pale to honey-colored; translucent to opaque

Patience / Serenity

How many times have you heard the expression "Rome wasn't built in a day?" Probably a lot. And it's the truth. Most things worth doing take a lot of time and patience if they are to be done right.

But what if patience just isn't a virtue you were born with? Try asking for help from a honey jade power bracelet. Besides providing you with calming and soothing energy, honey jade beads give you the ability to slow down and take time to enjoy the things that mean the most to you.

Cool Combo

Combine your honey jade with a rose quartz bracelet to develop the patience to build a strong romantic relationship.

India Agate

Green/Dark Red/Grey

multi-colored; translucent to mottled to opaque—
also known as Fancy Jasper

Motivation / Energy

Sometimes it's easy to get into a rut of doing absolutely nothing. It's comfortable to just sit and watch the world go by without you. You don't take any risks, so you're not in any danger of failing. But talk about wasting your potential! If you really want to make positive changes in your life, your school, your city, or even your planet, you've got to be motivated to get out there and do something. Make your mark!

Now's the time to get off the couch, turn off the tube, and slap on an India agate power bead bracelet. India agate is the motivation stone. It will help you develop the verve and energy needed to tackle even the toughest projects.

Cool Combo

To make your devotion to a good cause stick, wear your India agate beads alongside black onyx.

24

Lapis

Blue

bright to dark, sometimes speckled/mottled
with black, white, or gold; opaque

Communication/Self-Awareness

Has this ever happened to you? You know what you're trying to say, but your message just isn't getting through. No matter what words you use to describe your thoughts, your friends and family don't seem to have a clue. Sometimes you feel like you're playing that elementary school game "Telephone." Help is on the way! A lapis power bead bracelet can help you communicate your ideas more clearly to the people you are trying to reach.

Sometimes part of the problem with communicating an idea is that the concept isn't totally clear in your own mind. Lapis stones increase your self-awareness. They make your thoughts clearer, which makes it easier for you to communicate them to others simply and directly.

Cool Combo

Wear your lapis bracelet right beside your mother of pearl bracelet to help you communicate well in business.

White

shiny, sometimes mottled; translucent to solid

Wealth/Financial Confidence

Let's cut right to the chase. If you're looking for cash, mother of pearl is the power bead for you. This beautiful, white bead is often associated with prosperity and wealth. But don't think that the minute you put on a set of mother of pearl power beads money will start falling from the sky. What mother of pearl does is give you the confidence and business savvy that attracts investors. And that's where the money comes from.

Cool Combo

Wear your mother of pearl power beads with any other power beads to increase the energy from the other beads.

Orange & Yellow Wooden Beads

Orange/Yellow

natural wood color or dyed orange,
usually with small black printing on them
(often tiny Buddhas or Chinese); opaque

Harmony/Peace

Mala beads are not always made of semi-precious stones. Many of the most beautiful ones are made of carved wood. Orange and yellow wooden beads are among some of the most highly regarded power beads. That's because they are said to bring harmony into otherwise hectic lives.

Cool Combo

Wear the orange and yellow wooden beads together for a greater sense of inner peace.

Rock Crystal

Clear

crystal, usually with a red, green,
or white string; clear

Courage

Maybe the Wizard of Oz's Cowardly Lion would have found his courage sooner if he'd worn a power bead bracelet made from rock crystals. These clear stones provide you with the inner strength to tackle difficult tasks and to try new things. Being brave is what they are all about.

Cool Combo

Wear rock crystal beads with tiger's eye beads for increased creative confidence.

Rose Quartz

Pink
(of course!)
pale; translucent

Love / Romance

Of all the power bead bracelets out there these days, rose quartz may just be the most popular of all. And why not? People who are tired of waiting for Cupid to shoot his arrow in their direction are taking matters into their own hands—or, actually, their own wrists. Rose quartz opens your heart and mind to finding love. It brings peace to otherwise volatile relationships and helps heal wounded feelings. Why wait for Valentine's Day? Buy your love a rose quartz bracelet now, and watch the romance blossom.

Cool Combo

Wear rose quartz *mala* beads alongside lapis beads to help you communicate with your love.

Smokey Quartz

Grey/Brown
Dark but clear, like crystal mixed
with grey; translucent to clear

Relaxation

Wow! Wouldn't a massage feel good right about now? How about a hot bubble bath? Or what about a visit to the beach just to watch the waves come in?

There are lots of ways to relax. But not all of them are very practical when you have to go to school. So, for those times when you want to feel relaxed but you can't just run off to a spa, slip on a smokey quartz power bead bracelet. Smokey quartz has an energy source that will enhance your body's natural ability to simply chill out and calm down.

Cool Combo
For those times when you are extra-tense, combine smokey quartz with fluorite bracelets for an even greater calming influence.

Tiger's Eye

Gold/Brown/Black/Tan

Dark with swirls/stripes of gold/tan, shiny; opaque

Creativity / Artistic Ability

Who's the most creative person you can think of? Van Gogh? Shakespeare? Mozart?

How'd you like to add yourself to that list? Well, we can't guarantee that you'll be painting irises, writing sonnets, or composing symphonies, but we do know that many folks believe that tiger's eye beads enhance your natural creativity, by increasing your self-confidence.

Now you're probably wondering what creativity has to do with confidence. Well, did you ever watch a child draw? What may look like a series of scribbles to you looks like a masterpiece to the child. All children know they can draw. But over the years criticism of their artwork ("the sky isn't pink!") can start to inhibit a child's inner creativity. Tiger's eye beads can give you the confidence to release the artist within.

Cool Combo

Wear tiger's eye beads with mother of pearl bracelets to enhance your creative flow.

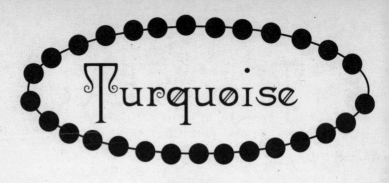

Turquoise

Blue

bright blue/turquoise, often speckled
with black, grey, or white; opaque

Healing/Problem Solving

While the energy in most gemstones affects only one specific issue, turquoise is a triple power bead. This blue-green gemstone is said to be able to heal physical aches in your body, while helping you to sort out and deal with problems that are weighing heavily on your mind, and spiritual questions that affect your soul. No other single stone appears to have so much healing power, although many gemstones can achieve similar effects when they are combined with other stones. A single strand of turquoise, however, can help heal the mind, body, and spirit. For that reason, turquoise is known as the master healer.

Cool Combo

Put on your turquoise power beads, then slide a bracelet made of fluorite beside them to replace your pain with calmness and serenity.

Party Power!

Question: What do you get when you bring your closest power bead lovin' friends together to eat scrumptious treats, make totally funky jewelry, and trade stories and bracelets?

Answer: A totally bead-ariffic party! Throwing a party is really fun. So is wearing power bracelets. Why not combine the two and throw a Power Bead Party?

Start with the Invitations

You don't have to go out and buy fancy invitations to your power bead party. You can make them yourself! Just buy some blank 3 x 5 cards and write the party info on them. Be sure to include the place, date, and time of your party. Decorate the invitations by gluing small, colorful, inexpensive plastic beads all over the cards. That way the bead fun gets started even before your friends arrive.

Bead Matching

Keep a box of beads by the front door. Make sure you have one bead for each girl, and only two beads in each color.

As each of your guests arrives, ask her to take one bead from the box. After everyone has arrived, tell each of your guests to walk around the room, and try to find another guest with the same color bead as she has.

Eventually, all of your guests will be paired off. Now each guest has an automatic buddy. Be sure not to give yourself a buddy. You already know everybody. And besides, you'll be needed to run the next game.

Once your pals have worked together to undo the tangled necklace, they'll be friends for life!

Tough Trivia

After your pals are paired off into teams of two, give each team a piece of paper and a pencil. Read the names of the different beads that are used to make power bracelets. Ask the teams to try and write down what effect each type of bead has on a person (what each bead means). Or, if you think that's too hard, ask the teams to tell you the color of the beads you name. The team that gets the most correct answers, wins. (A good prize might be a power bracelet for both girls on the winning team.)

Or here's another idea! You can try giving them the Power Bead Quiz which is on the next few pages.

Test Your Knowledge
The Ultimate Power Bead Quiz!

1 All right, here it is! It's the first day of school, and you want to make a good impression. You've got your new black jeans, your very cool boots, and a great red and gold top. You're all set to go! But you feel like there's one thing missing. You just need one extra magical addition to totally transform you into the coolest, most self-confident kid in school, so everyone will want to get to know you. Of course the answer is a power bead bracelet — but which one are you going to choose?

2 Uh-oh! Your best friend has missed two days of school because of the flu. If she doesn't get better soon, not only is she going to be stuck doing tons of homework for the rest of her life to catch up, but she's also going to miss your big party on Saturday night! Being a thoughtful and helpful friend, you of course bring her a box of cookies, and a bead bracelet with tons of healing power. Which two bracelets can you choose to give her for mighty flu relief?

3 You've met the guy of your dreams — he's sweet, he's smart, and he's so unbelievably cute. And best of all, he's still available! Plus, you have it on good

authority that he really digs girls who are brave enough to ask guys out themselves. Now all you need to do is work up the courage to do it! No problem, right? Well, perhaps this combination of two cool power bead bracelets will give you just the right mix of bravery and romantic vibes. What are they?

4 Your new friend who just moved in next door confides in you that she's always wanted to be a painter. You've seen some of her work, and you think she could be totally great. The problem is, she's too nervous to really work on her art — she has this idea that it might not be good enough to show anyone. There's an art competition coming up at school that you know she would love to enter, if she could just have faith in her creative ability. Of course you, with your amazing knowledge of power beads, realize there is the perfect power bead bracelet for this occasion, and you get it for her right away. Which one is it?

5 It's that most awful time of year again — finals week. You know you've studied like crazy and you can't imagine stuffing one more fact into your head. History, math, grammar — you know it's all in there somewhere. You just need something to keep you focused and help you remember everything clearly. Which power bead bracelet would be the ideal choice?

6 You and your best friend make a bet that you can both go an entire month without eating any chocolate at all. It's been three weeks, and you're doing great. But then your mom suggests that the family take a trip to the ice-cream store in town, to celebrate her promotion. Will you be able to go in there and NOT get a Triple Chocolate Chunk Monster Madness Death By Fudge Sundae? How will you ever be able to stop yourself? Clearly you need a special power bead bracelet to help you say no. Which one do you choose?

7 You and your boyfriend have had a fight — again. It's like no matter what you say, he takes it the wrong way! Your friends don't understand either — whenever you try to explain what you're fighting about, it comes out all muddled and confused. Which is kind of how you feel anyway! If only there were a way to explain to him how you feel. You just want to be able to present your thoughts logically and clearly — surely that can't be so hard! Well, what you obviously need is a bracelet to make your ideas clearer in your own head, so you can tell him (and your friends) exactly what you're thinking. Which bead bracelet would be perfect for you?

8 Your older sister absolutely loves her yoga class. She goes almost every day, and even you've noticed that she seems calmer and easier to deal with. After all, she has a really hectic life — basketball, homework, and the school newspaper, not to mention her after-school job and

that guy she's always with. So when she's stressed, it's kind of like the end of the world in your house! Then you find out that her yoga class is canceled for a whole week. What are you going to do? You know she's going to totally freak out if she doesn't find some way to meditate and calm down in the middle of her crazy schedule. She needs something that will help her think peaceful thoughts — very peaceful thoughts. To keep her from flipping out, which bracelet is the most perfect gift you could give her right now?

9 You've been saving up for weeks to get that amazing dress you keep seeing in the store window. It's perfect for you — just your color, and just the right size. But last week you had to spend some of your savings on two new power bracelets, because they're just so cool. Now you need cash fast, because this dress would be totally awesome for the big party this weekend. Nothing will make wealth just appear magically, but perhaps one of your bead bracelets can help you figure out a way to earn some quick money. Which one do you pick?

10 You have a huge crush on the guy who sits next to you in Spanish class. He's really adorable, and he always makes you laugh. Now, of course you've been wearing your rose quartz beads for love just about every day, but you think you'd have more luck getting his attention if there were only

something you could both work on together. Like, if you were both involved in some after-school activity, or some volunteer program…but after you do some digging, you find out that he's not involved in anything! Now, before you give up on this lazy guy, stop and think. Maybe all he needs is a little incentive — a little extra motivation to make him want to do something. You're cool enough to know that guys can wear bead bracelets just as well as girls, so the next day in class you casually give him one, mentioning that everyone in your community service club wears them, and maybe he'd like to come along to a meeting some day. You know that the beads you've given him will be just what he needs to get up and go, and then you can really get to know each other. Which motivating beads are these?

Answers to the Power Bead Quiz

Give yourself two points for each question you answered correctly. For questions with more than one answer, give yourself two points for each part of the question.

1. Clearly what is called for here is a **goldstone** power bead bracelet — to supercharge your positive attitude, match your awesome red and gold outfit, and make you totally ready to rule at school. Give yourself two points! (If you guessed green onyx, that will work too.)

2. What your friend needs is the healing energy of either a **hematite** or a **turquoise** bracelet. In fact, try bringing

her both, and watch the power make her full of good health and excitement, just in time for your party!

3. **Rose quartz** is definitely required for something as monumental as this — love energy that will hopefully have the same effect on him that it has on you! And for that extra dose of courage, try rock crystal for inner strength. Just feeling that cool combination on your wrist will totally prepare you for approaching Mr. Wonderful.

4. Slip your friend a **tiger's eye** bracelet, and you know she'll be entering that competition in no time. Not only will the beads give her the confidence to believe in her art, they will enhance her creativity and inspire her imagination.

5. Plan on wearing purple every day this week — it's time to power up that **amethyst** bead bracelet and sharpen your mental focus with the energy of intelligence. Those finals will be a total snap with these on your wrist!

6. The forces of **black onyx** power beads are just what you need for this challenge. It might be tough, so wear as many as you own! But with the energy of self-control they give you, you'll be able to win your bet, avoid the chocolate — and enjoy a Caramel Marshmallow Dreamboat Split instead.

7. Take a deep breath and slide on a cool **lapis** bracelet for help with communication. Now think about the problem. Doesn't everything make more sense now? With power beads like this, you'll feel energized to call him and explain things so well that he'll finally understand you! (This cool trick might work with parents, too — wouldn't it be nice to be on the same wavelength for once!)

8. It sounds like it's time to get your sister some **fluorite** beads. Their peaceful energy will hopefully help her meditate on her own, and keep her at least relatively calm. And the fact that you're offering her a gift, even if the power doesn't completely de-stress her, ought to at least deflect her anger from you for the rest of the week! For extra power, give yourself a point if you said honey jade for patience, hematite for serenity, or wooden beads for harmony. (You can give yourself a point for smokey quartz, too, although you know there's not a chance she'll ever actually relax!)

9. Obviously what you need is some **mother of pearl** power for some fast financial energy. Good thing you bought that bracelet last week! With the confidence it will give you, you might seek out those extra baby-sitting jobs — or get your dad to pay you for doing something around the house (like fixing the screen saver on his computer — he never can do it himself). You'll have that dress in no time — and fortunately mother of pearl goes with everything, so you can wear it to the party, too!

10. **India agate** is the stone of choice here. Not only is it cool-looking so even a guy can appreciate it, but it's got just the motivating energy you're looking for! Don't be surprised if he shows up at your next meeting — beads and all. Not only do you get to talk to him more now, but you'll also have transformed him into Mr. Energy! How cool is that?

Score Yourself!

20-24+ Bead Power Empress Wow! You are the Power Girl of All Beads! You've got the karma, and you know exactly what beads to use when. Were you wearing amethyst beads when you took this test?

14-20 Bead Power Queen You're definitely grooving — with your positive attitude (goldstone, anyone?) and knowledge of beads, you'll be ruling the bead world soon.

8-14 Bead Power Princess You're on the right track, but there's a lot to know about the perfect power beads for each situation. Maybe the triple power effect of some turquoise beads will help you figure them all out!

0-8 Bead Power Apprentice Well, it's a good thing you bought this book! Keep it with you for handy reference whenever you go bead shopping — until you have the confidence (try some aventurine!) to know instinctively whatever you're looking for.

Making Your
Own Beads

What would a power bead party be without the chance to make some beaded jewelry? Of course, buying enough power beads for each guest to make her own bracelet could get costly. So instead, why don't you and your friends make your own beads? These paper and clay bead bracelets may not offer the same healing powers as the actual wrist *mala*s do, but we guarantee they'll be every bit as beautiful and special.

Paper Beads

Here's what you'll need to make a paper bead bracelet:

- ⊘ triangles of brightly colored paper cut from glossy magazines. The triangles should be 1 1/2 inch wide at one end and 8 1/2 inches long. You will need about 15 triangles for each bracelet.
- ⊘ white glue
- ⊘ thin elastic thread
- ⊘ a pencil
- ⊘ coffee stirrers or toothpicks
- ⊘ flat watercolor paintbrushes
- ⊘ large-eyed needles
- ⊘ a small container for mixing the glue
- ⊘ wax paper

Here's how to make the paper beads and the bracelet:
1. Mix glue in a container with a small amount of water.

2. Use the paintbrush to spread a thin layer of glue on one side of a paper triangle. Cover the entire side of the triangle except for the first 3/4 of an inch at the broad end. Keep the glue just inside the long edges of the triangle.

3. Place the coffee stirrer or toothpick across the edge of the broad end of the triangle on the glue side. The stirrer will form the center core. Now roll the paper around the core. Continue to roll the core evenly toward the pointed end of the triangle, tightening the paper as you go along.

4. When you reach the point of the triangle, smooth it into place and wipe off any excess glue.

5. Slide the bead off of the coffee stirrer, and set it on the wax paper to dry.

6. Repeat steps 1 through 5 for each paper triangle.

7. When the beads are thoroughly dry, thread the needle with the thin elastic thread. Use enough thread to circle your wrist, plus an extra inch.

8. String the beads onto the elastic thread. When all the beads are strung onto the thread, knot both ends, leaving about half an inch of thread at each end. Tie the ends together with a knot to finish off the bracelet.

Clay Beads

Here's what you'll need to make clay beads and the bracelet:

- ⊘ 2 cups cornstarch
- ⊘ 4 cups baking soda
- ⊘ a measuring cup
- ⊘ a mixing bowl
- ⊘ 2 1/2 cups water
- ⊘ a pot
- ⊘ a dish cloth
- ⊘ wax paper
- ⊘ rolling pin
- ⊘ poster paints or acrylic paint
- ⊘ paintbrushes
- ⊘ coffee stirrers or toothpicks
- ⊘ plastic knife
- ⊘ thin elastic thread
- ⊘ large-eyed sewing needles

Here's how you make the beads and the bracelet:

1. Mix baking soda, cornstarch, and water in the pot.

2. (Ask an adult to) place the pot over medium heat on the stove and stir for four minutes until the mixture has thickened to the consistency of mashed potatoes.

3. (Ask an adult to) turn off the stove and remove the pot from the heat.

4. Cover the pot with a damp dishcloth, and allow the dough to cool.

5. Once the dough has cooled, knead it on a sheet of wax paper for five minutes.

6. Place the dough between two sheets of wax paper and use a rolling pin to roll the dough flat.

7. Pull off a piece of the dough and roll it into the shape of a bead.

8. Poke the coffee stirrer or toothpick through the bead to create a hole through which you can thread the elastic.

9. Gently slide the coffee stirrer out of the bead.

10. Place the bead on a piece of clean wax paper to dry.

11. Repeat steps 7-10 until you have formed enough beads to make your own bracelet.

12. Allow the beads to harden. (Be warned: This could take several hours.)

13. Use paint to decorate the beads.

14. When the paint is dry, thread the elastic through the needle. Use just enough elastic to encircle your wrist, plus one extra inch.

15. Once all of the beads are strung, knot the elastic at both ends, leaving one half inch of elastic on either side. Then tie the two ends together to finish off the bracelet.

Manicure Mania

Since wearing those fun and funky power bead bracelets will bring attention to your hands and wrists, why not spend some party time giving each other power manicures? Before the party, head over to your local drugstore and pick up some small sample-sized bottles of nail polish for your guests to use. Try to get colors that match the colors of your favorite power beads. A pale pink could be rose quartz. Turquoise nail polish would look really cool. Mother of pearl is always easy to find (brides wear it all the time!). Even green and black nail polish is sure to be available.

Once you've lined up all the colors you want, allow your guests to choose their faves. Also provide them with nail polish remover, cotton swabs, warm sudsy water, and nail files.

Now, here are a few manicure secrets from the experts: Remove all the old polish from your nails before you start—even the little bits that get caught around the edges. Always file your nails in one direction—upward from the corners to the tips. After you've finished filing, allow your nails to soak in warm sudsy water for a few minutes.

Once you're ready to polish your nails, take your time. Polish each nail with long strokes, making sure you polish up from the bottom of the nail. Allow the color to dry, then top with a coat of clear polish.

Check 'Em Off

Whether you buy them, make them, or trade them, by this point you probably have plenty of power bead bracelets. In fact, you might even have so many bracelets that it's almost impossible to keep track of all of them. So how do you know which bracelets you might still need?

We've solved that problem for you. Each time you get a new set of power beads, check them off on this list. Then you'll know which ones you need to buy, just so you can have them all.

- [ ] Amethyst
- [ ] Aventurine
- [ ] Black Onyx
- [ ] Fluorite
- [ ] Goldstone
- [ ] Green Onyx
- [ ] Hematite
- [x] Honey Jade
- [ ] India Agate
- [ ] Lapis
- [ ] Mother of Pearl
- [ ] Orange Wooden Beads
- [x] Yellow Wooden Beads
- [ ] Rock Crystal
- [x] Rose Quartz
- [ ] Smokey Quartz
- [ ] Tiger's Eye
- [ ] Turquoise